Piece of Cake

Without A Hitch

Book Three

By: Kent HamiIlton

Table of Contents

Chapter One 7

Chapter Two 14

Chapter Three 24

Chapter Four 28

Chapter Five 31

Chapter Six 39

Chapter Seven 47

Chapter Eight 49

© **Copyright 2020 by : KENT HAMILTON- All rights reserved.**

This document is geared toward providing exact and reliable information in regard to the topic and issue covered. The publication is sold with the idea that the publisher is not required to render accounting, officially permitted, or otherwise, qualified services. If advice is necessary, legal or professional, a practiced individual in the profession should be ordered.

- From a Declaration of Principles which was accepted and approved equally by a Committee of the American Bar Association and a Committee of Publishers and Associations.

In no way is it legal to reproduce, duplicate, or transmit any part of this document in either electronic means or in printed format. Recording of this publication is strictly prohibited and any storage of this document is not allowed unless with written permission from the publisher. All rights reserved.

The information provided herein is stated to be truthful and consistent, in that any liability, in terms of inattention or otherwise, by any usage or abuse of any policies, processes, or directions contained within is the solitary and utter responsibility of the recipient reader. Under no circumstances will any legal responsibility or blame be held against the publisher for any reparation, damages, or monetary loss due to the information herein, either directly or indirectly.

Respective authors own all copyrights not held by the publisher.

The information herein is offered for informational purposes solely, and is universal as so. The presentation of the information is without contract or any type of guarantee assurance.

The trademarks that are used are without any consent, and the publication of the trademark is without permission or backing by the trademark owner. All trademarks and brands within this book are for clarifying purposes only and are the owned by the owners themselves, not affiliated with this document.

Disclaimer:

The information presented in this book represents the views of the publisher as of the date of publication. The publisher reserves the rights to alter update their opinions based on new conditions. This report is for informational purposes only. The author and the publisher do not accept any responsibilities for any liabilities resulting from the use of this information. While every attempt has been made to verify the information provided here, the author and the publisher cannot assume any responsibility for errors, inaccuracies or omissions. Any similarities with people or facts are unintentional.

Chapter One

"I'm not going to make it."

His mother's words rang in his ears and echoed through his mind over and over again. John stared straight ahead at his mother's weak form, crumpled against the hospital wall. Her fingers seemed thin and veiny, clutching at a wad of used kleenex. She pressed a hand to her heart and offered her son a smile, but her eyes were not in it. They seemed distant, far off, as if she was looking at something years and years away from the bleak hospital with its white walls and linoleum floors.

"I'm not going to make it."

The words seemed to fill the empty, silent halls with darkness. Kari stared at John's mother as she stood, small and shaking, before them. She saw a woman she had come to love, had come to trust. She knew that John and his mother did not always get along, but in the last few months, their relationship had flourished. She had watched John's mother beam with pride at her son's strength, loyalty, and passion for life. Kari had shared secrets and tears with this woman, and she could not bare to think of going on without her warm and quirky presence. She glanced at John, and she could see in his eyes that he felt the same way.

"But..." Kari heard herself speaking, but the voice did not feel like it was her own. She swallowed and blinked, forcing herself to gain composure. "You will make it," she said, struggling to keep her voice from wavering. She tilted her chin upwards and stared John's mother firmly in the eye. "We're getting married, and you're going to be there," she said solidly, "and that is that."

John's mother chuckled softly, which set her off into a coughing fit. John stared in horror as his mother's body shook and shivered, wracked with the force of the coughs. Kari reached out a hand to steady the woman, but she brushed it away, proud as ever.

"I'm fine, I'm fine," she said, brushing tears from her eyes.

"If you're fine then I don't see any reason why you can't be at the wedding," John said fiercely. Kari looked at him sharply, shocked by the sharpness in his voice. She noted that his eyes were angry, but they shone with tears. She felt her hearty cry out in sympathy: her husband was angry at his mother's sickness, angry at the unfairness of life. He was hurting, and she felt his pain and wanted nothing more than to take him in her arms and hold him.

Instead, she chose to stand strong. Kari planted her feet and put a hand on John's mother's shoulder.

"It's going to be alright," she said, looking into the woman's distant eyes. "You are strong, and radiant, and the most stubborn person I know." A smile flashed across John's mother's lips. "If anyone can get through this, you can."

Kari felt John slide a hand around her waist, joining her at his mother's side.

"Kari's right, mom," John said, blinking the tears from his eyes. "You're stubborn as anything. I bet if you just told the sickness to get out of town, it would listen to you. I know that's worked for me before," he added, joking.

John's mother smiled fully and wrapped her arms around Kari and John.

"I appreciate the support," she whispered, her voice thin as paper, "I really do. But I don't think it's realistic to say everything is going to be alright. Not this time."

John's father's frame, tall and sturdy, filled the doorway of the hospital room. The man still appeared shaken, but he seemed to have regained some of his regular, solid composure.

"Son," he said. John looked up and nodded, following his father's eyes. In John's father's hands was a hospital issued clipboard. John walked over and took the clipboard in his hands. Kari watched as his eyes flitted over the page. Even in his distress, she was struck by how handsome her husband was. His blue eyes sparkled with kindness and empathy; his strong jaw worked as he whispered the words to himself. He was the man she had dreamed of, but dared not to believe in; he was her soul mate, the love of her life. She knew then that no matter how awful or difficult life became, and no matter what hardships the everyday threw their way, she and John, together, would always be able to pull through. They made each other stronger, more able- and she stood a little taller then, and wrapped her other arm around John's mother, for it was her job, she knew, to play the role of the pillar of strength in John's moment of need.

John finished inspecting the clipboard and dropped it to the floor. It clattered loudly in the silence of the hallway. He swallowed and his face became an ashen white grey. He rubbed his hands over his eyes and then through his hair, looking everywhere, looking nowhere.

John's father nodded and gripped his son's shoulder. Kari watched, holding John's mother closer to her, stroking her hair.

"John?" she asked. Her voice was gentle, soft. "John, what is it?"

He looked up, his blue eyes full of tears.

"It's a tumor," he said, and speaking the words made the tears in his eyes begin to fall. They streamed down his face freely, wetting his ruddy cheeks and making his nose run. He didn't seem to notice. "It's a tumor, and it's in her brain, and they've given her a week to live."

Kari felt her body go limp at the news. She struggled to maintain her embrace around John's mother, struggled to keep her lip from trembling. She felt cold, empty, and panicked all at once. She wanted to provide John with strength and love, but she was just as scared as he was. She had faced loss before, great, deep loss that had rocked her whole world and made everything come tumbling around her in glassy pieces; she had not been prepared to face it again, not so soon, not so deeply. John's mother was like a second mother to Kari. Kari's own mother had never been very close with her; they'd always had a pleasant enough relationship, but it was nothing more than a sort of putting up with each other. The way Kari had bonded with John's mother had provided her with so much love, joy, and affection. She had felt, for the first time in her life, that she had a mother/daughter bond like something out of a book, or a movie. The way she and John's mother spoke, laughed, and connected felt magical. She wasn't ready to lose that. She didn't want to lose that.

Kari let go of John's mother, giving her one last squeeze before she walked over to her husband's side. She wrapped her arms around John and he collapsed against her shoulder, sobbing and shaking with grief.

"Hey John, hey," she cooed, running a hand softly through his hair. "I'm here. I'm here." John wrapped his arms around Kari and pulled her closer. "It's alright," she whispered into his ear, then quickly amended her comforting words. "It's awful," she admitted, tears slipping into her own eyes, "but I'm here for you, and we've got each other. And we're going to be here with your mom, to see that she has everything she needs for her final days. She's going to be comfortable, and happy, and loved. She's going to feel all the things that her son makes me feel." Kari pulled back and placed her hands on John's cheeks. She wiped the tears from his eyes and stood on tip toes to kiss the top of his head.

"I know," John said. He looked at his mother, who was now leaning against his father, beginning the slow walk down the badly lit hallway, back to her hospital room. "I know. I just wanted her to see us get married. That's the only thing she ever wanted- to see me get married- and now she'll never get that," John said. His voice broke and fresh tears began to slide down his cheeks.

Kari stared at her husband, and something suddenly clicked in her mind. Her heart leapt and she pulled her cell phone out of her pocket.

"I think that we can still make that happen," she said, quickly dialing Mary's number and pressing the phone to her ear.

John shook his head.

"You heard her. There isn't time. Even if we waited we'd only be waiting for her to be dea-" Before he could finish the sentence, John was wiping the tears from his eyes again.

Kari looked at her husband, her face alive with hope. She listened to the dial tones in her ear. Each one made the butterflies in her stomach jump a little more, because each one brought her closer and closer to making her idea a reality.

"John," she said, cupping his face in her hand. "Look at me, John."

John's blue eyes poured into her hazel eyes and she felt the wave of love and warmth pass over her as it always did. She smiled, and he smiled too, even through his tears.

"I love you, John," she said.

"I love you too, Kari," he said. His face clouded over again as he swatted the tears from his eyes. "But I feel awful that my mother will never see me married."

"Oh, I think she will," Kari said. John looked up in confusion. "Come on, John," said Kari, "we've gotten married in a hospital before. Don't you think we can manage it again?"

Chapter Two

At 7:00 am the next morning, John's mother returned to her hospital room. She was weak, tired, and sick from the chemotherapy she had just undergone. Yet she still had enough energy to reprimand the nurse who accompanied her.

"That's the last I'm doing that!" she barked angrily as the nurse helped her into bed. "It's stage four and it's in my brain and I've heard how these things go. There's absolutely no point in you making me vomit out my insides for the course of my last seven days on this earth!"

The nurse tucked the blankets beneath her patient's head and nodded in understanding.

"That's a fair decision," she said, "and I'll see to it that your wishes are enacted. You have that right."

John's mother nodded in satisfaction, glad to have gotten her way. She was about to let her eyes fall shut and slide away into a fitful sleep when she caught a glimpse of something out of the corner of her eye.

"What's that?!" she snapped, pushing herself up in an attempt to get out of bed. The nurse hurried to help her back under the covers.

"Please, you must rest," she said nervously. John's mother obliged- but she refused to give up her query of questions.

"What is that, young lady?" she demanded, raising a weak hand to point at the banquet table that had been set up against the right wall of her room, beneath the window. The table was covered in a light blue cloth of satin, and decorated with flowers painted gold.

"Oh, that...." the nurse said, stuttering uneasily. "It's... why.... It's.... Oh it's nothing."

But even as she said the words, two men pushed open the door of the hospital room. John's mother watched in shock as they carried in tray after tray of stunningly decorated cupcakes and set them upon the table. She wiggled around in her bed, craning her neck to get a better look.

"Now I've been around a while," she began as the men returned, now toting hot plate after hot plate, "and I know something when I see it. This, young lady, is certainly not nothing. This," John's mother said, looking indignantly at the nurse, "is very much of a something."

The nurse flushed and wrung her hands.

"Please, I've promised," she begged. "Please, don't make me spoil it. Please go to sleep, ma'am. Please."

But sleep was out of the question: more men were now pouring into John's mother's room. Three of them got to work setting up an iron arch laced with green trellises and white flowers; two more men set stools upon the floor and began to hand crystal lights from the ceiling; another man rolled a red carpet across the floor and began to dust it with rose petals. John's mother pursed her lips and shot her eyebrows up her forehead, looking excitedly at the nurse.

"Oh I don't think you have to say anything at all, darling," she began, casting her eyes over the scene. She pulled at her blankets and fluffed up her pillows, giving herself a comfortable seat to watch the action. "And don't you worry- I'm disgustingly exhausted, and I am going to sleep. But don't think I don't know what's going on here." With that, John's mother closed her eyes.

The young nurse flushed and her bottom lip began to quiver.

"I am so sorry for ruining the surprise," she said. "Oh, I am so sorry for ruining your day."

John's mother cracked one eye open and squinted at the nurse.

"Ruining my day? Silly girl," she tutted. She closed both her eyes again and grinned. "This is about to be the best day of my life."

~

The church across from the hospital clanged out the hour. The brass bells rang, strong and clear, twelve times, announcing the arrival of midday.

Inside the hospital room, John's mother lay in a peaceful, fitful sleep. Despite her best efforts to stay awake and oversee the setting up of things, she had drifted to sleep mere seconds after her nurse had left her; chemotherapy was hard on the body, and her body was weak and tired. Sleep had fallen over her like a warm blanket, and she had been glad to succumb to its quiet and rejuvenation.

While she slumbered, the men had worked their magic. The hospital room had been transformed into a place of beauty, whimsy, and fairy tale delight. Rose petals lay across John's mother's blankets, decorating her sleeping form in gentle elegance. Cupcakes, their candles flaming, stood guard upon the satin draped banquet table. The hanging crystal lights caught the daylight that fell through the open windows, and reflected glittering splashes of color across the hospital room. Flowers lined the makeshift, red carpet aisle; brilliant bouquets of crocuses, lilacs, and sunflowers stood in tall vases, marking the walk to the iron arch. The arch stood proudly, and the trellises and flowers that clung to it swayed ever so slightly in the warm breeze that spilled in through the open window. The hot plates hummed with the promise of delicious catered food. The room waited in silent beauty for the wonder that was about to begin.

Outside the hospital, Kari took a deep breath. She ran her hands through her hair one last time, checking her reflection in the side of the car door. She stifled a giggle as she caught a glimpse of herself in the white dress. She'd worn it the last time she'd got married, and slipping it on had washed her in a wave of emotions. But today, she felt positively giddy in her wedding gown. Wearing it made her feel as if Mark was here, with her, smiling and giving her his approval. Yes, the dress was a bit more snug around the middle than it had been the first time she'd worn it- but that was just a reminder that there was life growing inside of her. The first time she'd worn this dress, it had marked the first day of a love that had given birth to the child she now carried in her womb. Wearing it now, she couldn't help but wonder excitedly at what her life with her John would prove to have in store.

The church bells across the street tolled out the twelfth ring, marking the hour for what it was.

"Go time," Kari whispered to herself, and she took one final breath, and walked confidently up the steps and through the front doors of the hospital.

As she walked through the lobby, she felt the eyes of patients and their families fall upon her. She couldn't help but smile- her, dressed in full make up, her hair curled artfully around her heart shaped face, her one thousand dollar dress trailing across the linoleum floor. As she passed the nurse's table, she caught John's mother's nurse's eye, and she couldn't help it. Kari burst out laughing, and the nurse was quick to join. It felt good to laugh, so Kari let herself take joy in the moment. She let her laughter take her to a place of happiness and contentment, the emotions she'd always imagined she would feel on her wedding day, the emotions that John and his family had bathed her in, every day since they had come into her life.

By the time she reached the elevators, Kari's face hurt from grinning, and her stomach ached from laughing. She felt the baby inside of her moving, and she placed a hand atop the shiny white material, lovingly patting the child within her.

"Apparently I'm not the only one who's excited," Kari said to the nurse. The nurse giggled.

"You should have seen your mother in law this morning," she told Kari. "I thought she was going to murder me, but I guess it was just her way of showing how happy she was about today."

Kari burst out in a fresh fit of laughter.

"Yes, that sounds exactly like her!" she said. She pressed the button for Floor 5 and the elevator soared upwards.

The doors opened on the first floor, revealing an assembly of finely dressed people, all waiting to receive Kari. Mary's hands fluttered to her mouth as she took in the sight of her best friend.

"My goodness," she gasped. "You look more radiant than ever, Kari! And that's saying something, you beautiful girl!"

Kari laughed and gripped her friend's arm fondly.

"Speak for yourself, you wonderful thing, you," she said. "I can never thank you enough for all the work you put into this. Organizing everything, getting all those people to donate that food, making sure all the cupcakes arrived on time--"

"Oh, shush, you," Mary said jokingly, waving a hand at Kari. "It was nothing at all. Just a few phone calls. You're the one who made all those cupcakes last night- each one of them unique! I don't know who you are, Kari Goodbar, but I'm quite sure you must be some sort of a superwoman."

Kari blushed and looked at her feet.

"I don't think so," she said shyly. "I think I just really like baking. It's my favourite thing in the world- and it led me to the man who has made me the happiest woman in the world." As she said the words, Kari realized, for the first time, just how beautiful this circumstance was. "Oh, Mary, I'm so grateful. I'm so happy to have you, and all these other lovely people, in my life."

Mary wiped a tear from her eye and grinned at her friend.

"And we're so grateful for you, Kari," she said. "But come on! Enough with the corny comments! We've got a marriage to make happen, and you're not going to be late for your own wedding! Not on my watch!" And she grabbed Kari's hand and began running down the hall giggling, giddy as a little girl.

The two friends careened down the linoleum floors, laughing as their high heels clacked against the tiles. They turned the corner and slid bang into the chests of Caleb, and John.

"Nooooo!" Mary squealed. "You guys can't see each other! It's bad luck for the bride and groom to see each other before the wedding!" She threw her hands over Kari's eyes.

"Um, Mary?" Kari giggled. "John and I are already married."

Kari felt Mary's hands fall from her eyes.

"Oh," she said, her cheeks reddening. "Right. I guess that's right." She grinned sheepishly up at John and Kari. "Sorry, friends; I keep forgetting it's wedding part two!"

John laughed and patted Mary on the shoulder.

"Don't you worry," he said. "I'm just thankful for all you've done to set up a wedding over night!"

"Now don't you start getting all corny too!" Mary teased, shaking a scolding finger at John. Just then Rod poked his head out of John's mother's hospital room.

"Hey, guys?" he called in a stage whisper. They all turned to look at him. "It's show time."

John adjusted his pocket kerchief. Caleb cleared his throat. Mary moved a hair out of Kari's eyes. Kari felt the butterflies begin to dance about her stomach again.

"Maybe it isn't butterflies," she thought suddenly, "but rather the baby, cheering us on." This thought made her warm inside, and she smiled, excited to be married, again.

John leaned forward, his lips brushing tenderly against her ear.

"Doubly married," he whispered. "That's fitting."

"How do you mean?" she asked.

"I love you so much, one wedding wasn't enough," he replied, smiling. She laughed and kissed him lightly on the cheek.

Rod's head disappeared back inside the room for a moment, then quickly popped out of the door again.

"Alright!" he called. "Let's go!"

Kari looked at John.

"I'm suddenly nervous," she said.

John laughed.

"Why?" he asked, his eyebrows arching up his forehead. "We're already married, honey."

"I know," Kari said, "but I want it to be perfect. For your mom."

It was as if a storm cloud passed across John's face- for a moment, Kari thought her husband was going to cry. But the moment lasted just a millisecond, and then John was back, grinning, excited, as enthusiastic and happy as ever.

"It will be perfect," he told Kari. He ran a finger fondly across her lips. He wondered how they could be so perfect, so pink and lovely. "You're perfect for me, and you've made our lives perfect, and so all this can be is perfect, Kari." He squeezed Kari's hand.

Rod rolled his eyes.

"Yea yea, great! You're in love! We get it. Let's go!"

Kari glanced nervously at John.

"See you out there?" she asked timidly.

John nodded reassuringly.

"See you out there."

Chapter Three

Rod pushed open the door, and Kari stepped in.

The heels of her shoes sunk into the lush red carpet. She looked up and gasped at the room's transformation. What had been a depressing, bleak hospital room yesterday was now a magic, fantasy world of cupcakes, flowers, and crystals. As Keri's eyes drifted over the candles sparkling from each of her one hundred unique cupcakes, her breath caught in her throat and she thought she would cry. She swallowed and shook her head, a smile replacing the tears that had threatened to well up in her eyes. It was magical, beautiful, as close to perfect as anything ever could be. She took a step forward, sunflowers to her left, crocuses to her right, both of them waving her on with beauty and pride.

As she took her third step towards the flower encircled iron arch, she noticed John's mother stir in her bed. Kari's mother in law rubbed the sleep from her eyes and sat up, and her movement caused rose petals to tumble from the sheets of her blankets and all across the floor. As Kari watched, she couldn't help but think that it seemed as if she was watching a fairy queen waking from a dream.

John's mother's eyelids fluttered, and then her eyes opened fully and she saw Kari. Her mouth dropped open and she sat up, very straight, in her bed. Before her stood her daughter in law, walking gracefully as a dancer across the red carpet covered in rose petals. Her hair was curled and pinned high upon her head, tiny strands breaking free from the twist and falling to kiss her cheekbones and frame her forehead in hazel locks. Kari's eyes sparkled with joy, and her lips were twisted into the prettiest, fullest pink smile. And her dress- her dress. Kari's dress slid off her shoulders in silky folds, curving to perfectly hug her body, baby bump and all. The satiny white material caught the light reflected by the hanging crystals, and appeared to dance and sparkle with every step Kari took. Beads of glittering emerald had been stitched into the skirt of the dress, and they caught the sunlight that trickled in through the window and sparkled as Kari walked down the aisle. Her veil tumbled down across her back and a sprig of lilac pricked its flowered head from behind her left ear. As Kari reached the arch and moved to stand beneath it, John's mother couldn't help but smile and blink the tears from her eyes. This was everything she had ever dreamed of- watching her son marry a girl who was truly beautiful, inside and out.

John walked the aisle next, followed by Mary, Caleb, and Rod. He beamed as he strode toward his bride, his hair slicked back stylishly, his suit fitted and cuffed just above the ankles to show off his lucky plaid socks. When he joined Kari under the arch, he squeezed her hand. John's mother watched as her son's eyes danced when they hit Kari's. It was a moment she had waited for for her entire life.

The vows were as beautiful as they had been when Kari and John had rehearsed them in John's parents' house, next door. Kari stifled a laugh as she caught John's mother's lips moving along with her own as she recited her vows- John's mother had actually committed the vows to memory! John rolled his eyes teasingly, and his mother tsked and laughed.

"And now," the priest said, closing his book, "you may kiss the bride."

John reached forward and ran his hands along the sides of Kari's face. He cupped her cheeks in his palms and gazed into her eyes.

"Hey you?" he whispered as he leaned forward. His lips felt like butterflies against her cheek, and Kari absentmindedly placed a hand upon her tummy. "I really love you," John said. Then he pressed his lips to her own.

John's mother clapped and the nursing staff cheered as the bride and groom kissed beneath the flower laden arches.

"And now," John announced, spreading his arms wide in welcome. "Can we please eat?!"

Everyone laughed, and Kari threw her arms around her husband.

"See?" he whispered in her ear as everyone fumbled for plates and food. "I told you my mom would love it."

Kari shook her head, beaming.

"It's beyond perfect," she said. She looked up at her husband, rose petals in her cheeks. "It's beyond a dream come true."

He nodded, and squeezed her hand.

"I think my mom thinks so, too. Look," he gestured. Kari followed John's gaze towards the bed, where his mother sat, a plate of three beautiful cupcakes upon her lap. The nursing staff were gathered around her bed side, nodding and cooing as she spoke.

"...and this one has a butterfly made of marzipan on top," John's mother was saying. She lifted the purple cupcake high in the air, showing it off to all that could see. "Did you know people could even do that- make butterflies that you can eat, all just out of marzipan? That's talent, that's what that is. That's my daughter in law, who made them. Do you know anyone so talented?!"

Kari blushed as she overheard John's mother's words. John wrapped an arm around her fondly.

"That's my girl," he said, and he kissed Kari again, warmly, passionately, his blue eyes sinking into her brown eyes.
Deep inside her, Kari swore she felt the baby dance for joy.

Chapter Four

After the festivities had died down, and the nursing staff had returned to work, Kari sat at the foot of her mother in law's bed, sipping sparkling juice and talking.

"It was perfect," John's mother kept saying, over and over again. "You both looked so beautiful, and so happy. It was so, so, absolutely perfect. And I wouldn't say that lightly."

Kari just smiled. She was warm, and full, and pleased. Everyone had raved about her cupcakes; her husband was a beautiful, loving man; her mother in law had been able to get the wish of her lifetime granted before her death. There was a certain unspoken sadness that hung in the air, but Kari refused to speak of it right now. Right now, the moment was perfect, and she wanted to sit inside this second forever.

John's mother coughed slightly and a look of exhaustion passed over her face.

"Honey?" she asked Kari. "Could you get a nurse for me, honey? And I don't mean to be a bother, but could we get the room cleared out? I'm just so very tired from that pesky radioactive business."

Kari nodded and pushed herself up of the bed, one hand upon her stomach.

"Absolutely," she replied. She turned to go, then stopped and bent forward to plant a light kiss upon her mother in law's cheek.

"Thank you," she said. "For welcoming me into your family. For... for everything."

Kari watched as John's mother's eyes drifted away again, into that far off place.

"It is my pleasure, Kari," she said, her voice soft and slow, "and you've given me and my family more joy than you will likely ever know." She squeezed Kari's hand weakly, and her eyes fluttered shut. Kari smiled and walked down the hallway to call one of the nurses to the hospital room.

When she returned with a nurse in tow, Kari was greeted by the sound of a solid unbroken, droning beep. She felt suddenly cold and sick, and rushed through the room to find John standing at his mother's bedside, his arm linked through his father's, tears running down his cheeks.

"She's gone," he said. Kari wrapped her arms around her husband and her father in law and the three adults broke into silent tears. They gripped each other, pulling each other closer and closer, and cried until they couldn't cry any longer. They pulled apart from each other's arms, and looked fondly at John's mother's lifeless form, lying upon the bed.

"Look at that," John's father said, his voice cracking. He chuckled through his tears. "She's got a smile on her face."

Kari and John looked at the small, frail body, comfortably resting upon the white hospital sheets. Sure enough, the tips of her thin lips were curled upward in a permanent smile.

"She never smiled like that until you came into my life," John said absentmindedly, gripping at Kari's gown. Kari nuzzled John fondly.

"She's smiling now, forever," she said. She wiped a tear from her eye.

"She died the happiest she has ever been," John's father confirmed. He bent to grab his wife's hand. "And I loved her, every minute of it all." He looked to his son and daughter in law. "I guess I'd like a moment to be with my wife. And son, you can have a moment with yours."

John nodded, and he and Kari walked slowly out of the room.

Chapter Five

Kari stood at the window, watching the cars drive by. So many thoughts ran through her head. It had been two months since John's mother had died. Things had been sad, but as a family, she, John, and his father had been able to pull through, and make the best of things. Kari stood now, watching the cars rush down the street through the light summer rain, her hands resting on her stomach. She was due in a month, and she could feel the child inside her pushing to break free of her womb. She rubbed a hand over her stomach soothingly, hoping to relax her baby.

"I know, I know," she muttered softly. "You want to get out here, and see the world. But things can be hard out here, little guy." She sighed and brushed the hair back from her eyes and behind her ear. "So you should enjoy your time there, in the safety, while you can."

The rain fell down the window pane in pretty rivulets. Kari watched and thought idly about John. She wondered how his lesson was going. Despite the rain, John's 11:00 student had refused to cancel his lesson, and so John was now out on the courts, working on the child's serve as the rain tumbled gently around them. She smiled at the thought of John, his dark hair plastered to his forehead with moisture, his blue eyes squinting through the rain drops to inspect his student's form. John was loving, caring, and nurturing- all the things a great father should be. Kari could not be happier with her husband. And yet here she was, drenched in melancholy, staring at the rain as it snaked down the windowpane.

The child kicked and Kari stumbled back slightly from the impact.

"Woah," she laughed, "that was a pretty fierce kick there, kiddo." She rubbed at her stomach and felt the little feet moving beneath the skin. It never ceased to amaze her- that there was a real, live, tiny human just beneath the surface of her flesh, living and breathing and waiting to come enter the world, out of her. She shook her head in awe and walked across the room to the kitchen, where she refilled her cup of coffee and leaned against the counter.

In the last week, as the due date grew closer and closer, Kari's thoughts had circled around memories of her late husband, Mark. She had woken up a few nights ago and thought it was Mark, not John, sleeping beside her. When she had remembered her reality, she had not felt upset; rather, confused, out of place, and slightly anxious. She loved John ferociously and passionately, and there was truly no one else with whom she could imagine herself spending the remainder of her days. Yet that night, at two am, as the moonlight spilled through the open window and pooled in her lap upon the bed, she felt uneasy. There was a child inside of her, and it was not John's child- it was Mark's child. Part of her wished she could snap her fingers and make the baby John's genetic son; part of her clung to the fact that Mark lived on, through this small life that was, each and every day, coming closer and closer to being a reality. And there Kari sat, between these two fierce emotions, unsure which she loved more, uncertain as to which thought was, to her, more true: did she want this child to be John's? Or did she forever want to hold onto Mark?

And then there were Kari's fears. She sipped at her coffee and ran a hand absentmindedly over her stomach, her brow creasing as her mind fogged with her familiar worries. What if the child was born, and it looked exactly like Mark? What if it only made her think of how much she missed her late husband? What if every day spent with the child was grievous and painful, to the point where she found herself despising the child she had always dreamed of loving? Or what if John and the child did not get along? What if she loved the child more than she could even possibly imagine, and in her loving of the child, neglected her husband? What if she was a horrible mother?

Kari shook her head, cleansing her mind of these thoughts. They were annoying, bothersome worries that had the tendency to cloud her brain when she was alone. She wished John's lesson would hurry up and end so he could come home and convince her of how unfounded and silly her thoughts were. 'Those are just normal worries,' he'd say, kissing her forehead and running his hands through her hair. 'It's going to be okay. It's all good. Everything is going to be okay.'

Kari sighed and placed the empty coffee cup back on the counter. She suddenly felt spasms of pain in her stomach, and gripped the edge of the sink to steady herself.

"Oh!" she gasped, biting down on her lip to distract herself from the pain. Her lower stomach felt as if it was buckling in on itself. She took a few deep breaths, in through her nose, out through her mouth, but it did nothing to quell the pain in her stomach. She turned and walked, slowly and carefully, one hand pressed to her womb, across the kitchen and into the living room. She lowered herself down onto the couch and turned she could lay upon her back. She pressed both hands onto her lower abdomen and stared up at the ceiling, breathing slowly.

Kari heard the key in the lock, twisting back and forth as John worked to let himself in. Then she heard the door open and close, and the sound of John's running shoes being kicked against the wall and bouncing onto the floor.

"Hey, honey!" His voice was like a beacon. She never got tired of hearing his "Hey honey"s echo throughout the house each time he got home. John's voice was deep, warm, and comforting. It sounded like a summer night filled with beach side bon fires; it made her feel like it was winter time and she was wrapped in a woolen blanket, in front of a fire, sipping hot chocolate and listening to Christmas carols. John was a slice of sunlight, a bit of radiance that added life and color to her everyday existence.

He wandered into the living room and stopped when he spied her lying on her back upon the couch.

"Hey," he said, his voice colored with concern. "Are you okay, Kari, honey?"

Kari breathed out slowly and tried to smile, but the pain turned her smile into a grimace.

"I think I'll be fine," she said, glancing at her husband and scowling at the pain that followed her movement. "It just really hurts right now."

John squatted next to Kari, and placed a hand upon her tummy. His eyes widened and his eyebrows shot up his forehead.

"Wow," he commented, patting her stomach. "The little guy's going crazy in there."

Kari arched an eyebrow and breathed in.

"We don't know if it's a guy, John, remember that," she said. Her tone came out more irritated than she had intended.

John stood up and looked at her.

"Hey," he said. "Are you mad at me?"

Kari sighed and shook her head. She looked down at her stomach.

"No," she said. "No I'm not. I'm mad at me."

John moved the pillows from the foot of the couch and sat down next to his wife.

"Hey," he said, placing her feet upon his lap. He began to massage them slowly and tenderly. "What's going on?"

Kari felt tears bite at her eyes and she sniffed.

"I don't know why I'm so emotional," she said, fighting to keep herself from crying, "and I don't want to make you feel like I don't love you. Because I do. My goodness, I do, John; I love you so much."

"Hey, I know that, honey," John said, giving her ankles a gentle squeeze. "Don't you ever worry about that, ever. I love you so much, too, Kari, and nothing could change that."

Kari smiled through her tears and then gasped in pain. John ran a hand over her lower abdomen, attempting to soothe the spasms.

"I guess...I just keep thinking about Mark," she breathed, watching John's face. He remained calm and understanding. He was such a good, good man. "I miss him, obviously. I mean I did love him, and of course I miss him..."

John nodded and placed his hand on top of her own.

"Of course you miss Mark," he said, looking into his eyes. His blue eyes were so bright, so calming, like the sea on the bluest of summer days. "You loved him. And you're carrying his child. And I will be a father to this child, absolutely, and I will raise him and love him like my own. But he is Mark's child, and so you're probably feeling torn and confused and a little sad that Mark can't see this. And that's healthy, honey. And that's natural. And I'm here for you, through all of that."

Kari breathed out a huge rush of air. She hadn't realized she'd been holding her breath, but the sigh left her feeling more relaxed, less tense. She reached up a hand and ran her fingers over John's face. He laughed as she accidently poked him in the nose.

"Ew," she said, giggling. He leaned over and kissed her sweetly upon the lips.

"Don't you worry," he said. "Everything is going to be okay."

She grinned up at him and for a moment, everything was right. John's blue eyes poured their sea spray color into her her hazel, tree bark eyes. Blue and brown danced and sparkled in loving unity. Then all of a sudden Kari screamed.

John jumped up and yelped in reaction to his wife's own pained gasping.

"What! Kari, what! What is it!"

Kari shoved herself into a sitting position and grabbed at her stomach, staring at John. Her face was white as a sheet and her eyes were masked with terror.

"John," she gasped, "John. John."

John nodded, gripping at her fingers.

"Yes, Kari. Kari, I'm here. What is it."

Kari took a breath and yelped out again.

"John. Call a cab. My water broke."

"What?" John's fingers fumbled for his cell phone as beads of sweat popped up along his forehead.

"My water broke, John. John, I'm having the baby."

Chapter Six

John gripped Kari's hand in his own as they rode through the rain towards the hospital. Every few minutes, Kari's face would squeeze up in pain and she would moan or scream, grasping John's hands so tightly that her knuckles would turn white. John rubbed her back and kept telling her in a soft voice, "Everything is ok. Everything will be just fine. You're doing great." But inside his mind, John felt just as frightened as Kari. He wanted to be strong and stable, to provide his wife with the comfort and reassurance she deserved. But he had no idea what this would be like. He didn't know why the baby was coming so early. He had heard horror stories about premature babies, and he didn't want anything to happen to his wife, or to his child to be. He felt distant, as if he was floating outside of his body, observing the panic from far, far away. He wanted it all to be over; he wanted to be calm and safe and holding his wife and their child. He didn't want the fear, the worry, the mania that now engulfed him. He kept his eyes on Kari's face, and made sure his lips kept cooing helpful, comforting words. He wished he felt as calm and collected as he knew he sounded.

The car pulled into the hospital and John scooped Kari up into his strong, tan arms. He carried her across the parking lot, through the rain. The rain had grown heavier and it soaked through their clothing and ran down their faces in rivulet as John jogged across the parking lot towards shelter. Kari grabbed at his shirt and writhed in pain as they entered the hospital.

"We need help!" he yelped without even thinking, and nurses immediately turned their way. Their mouths dropped open and they gaped at the sight of the two rain soaked people, fear riding their faces.

"She's having a baby," John said, hugging his wife to him. Then he stopped and looked at one of the nurses. "We're having a baby," he said, and for the first time, he truly realized what was about to happen: he was about to have a child. He was about to become a father. His entire life was about to change, forever. He had walked into this hospital as a man, but he would be leaving with an entirely new identity. He would be leaving as a role model, a guardian, a teacher, an advisor... It all overwhelmed him and he was promptly sick.

He threw up and Kari leapt from his arms to avoid the vomit. One of the nurses rushed forward and helped Kari into a wheel chair, while another nurse handed John a napkin and a cup of water before setting to clean the floor. Then they ushered John and Kari down a hallway and into a hospital room. The whole thing was a blur to John. He saw Kari on the table, the hospital gown draped around her shoulders, the doctor instructing her to breathe deeply while measuring her dilation. John felt useless and out of place, as if he was watching a medical show on television. He finished his cup of water and clutched dumbly at the cup for a few moments, staring, mouth open, at the scene playing out before him. Then Kari screamed again and the doctor said, "We are ready, people!"

This woke John up from his fogged brain haze. He jumped back to life, and back into reality. He rushed across the room, letting the paper water cup fall to the floor. He grabbed his wife's hand and looked into her eyes.

He was there now. He was committed. He had had every chance to walk out, and he admitted, something in him and almost wanted to. Almost. But he didn't want to walk out- not now, not ever. He wanted to be exactly where he was- here, beside Kari, holding her hand, seeing her through, now and forever.

Kari's head turned and she squinted up at John through the pain. Beads of sweat rolled down her face and tears dotted her eyes. Her pupils were glassy from the pain killers the nurses had given her.

"John..." she slurred, gripping his hand in her own. John squeezed her hand back.

"You can do this," he said, his eyes filling with loving tears. "Oh, Kari, God, I love you so much. You're going to have this baby and everything is going to be alright."

Kari's eyes fluttered opened and closed and she smiled for a brief second. Then her face squelched up in pain again and she screamed.

"Push!" the doctor called, and he motioned to John to encourage Kari.

"Come on, Kari," John said, sweat running down his own brow. "Push, push, push."

Kari squeezed her husband's hand so hard John lost feeling in his fingers. But he did not break eye contact with his wife.

"I...can't..." Kari puffed, tears streaming down her face.

"Yes, you can," John said, running his free hand through his wife's hair. "Yes you can, Kari."

Kari looked at him, then pushed hard, screaming out.

The doctor yelped and grabbed at the baby as it began to make it entrance into the world.

"Keep pushing!" John cried, watching as he saw a tiny leg appear. "Keep pushing!"

Kari gasped and yelped as she pushed, hard, one last time. Then she fell back upon the table, sweating, breathing hard, her eyes rolling back from the effort.

The doctor appeared from behind the curtain with a small pink bundle in his arms. He held up the baby- their baby.

"Kari, John," he said. "It's a girl."

John broke into tears and reached out for his baby girl. She was beautiful. She had tiny grey green eyes, like Mark had had, and a little pink mouth that looked just like Kari's. He passed her to Kari and Kari smiled, tears running down her face. She kissed her baby upon the forehead and held her close.

"She's beautiful," Kari gasped, and John nodded.

"Yes, she is. You were right. Not a boy," he said.

Kari nodded.

"We'll have to pick a new name," she mumbled, drifting off towards sleep.
"Yes, we will," John said. He watched his wife's face slide towards peacefulness. Then, suddenly, her face squeezed up again and she began to shake.

"Kari?" John jumped to her side in concern. She handed him the baby and pushed herself back up into a sitting position. "Kari!" John yelled.

The doctor rushed over and stared.

"She's still having contractions," he mused in utter shock. "Wait a second... wait a second..." The doctor drew his stethoscope from his neck and slammed it against Kari's stomach. His eyes grew to the size of saucers and his eyebrows soared so high up his forehead that John swore they would jump off his head entirely. "There's another heartbeat," the doctor said. He yanked the stethoscope off and slipped fresh rubber gloves onto his hands. "There's another baby."

John's face tumbled into an expression of disbelief.

"What?" he said. "How is that possible?"

The doctor shook his head.

"It's smaller than the first one, I think, but it's definitely in there, and it is definitely coming." He got ready to receive the baby, and pressed a hand against Kari's stomach. "Alright, Mom, just a few more minutes here, alright?" he said, coaxingly. "You're doing great. Just one more time. You can do it!"

"Okay honey, push! Push!" John's mind raced with thoughts as he held his daughter to his chest. Two children? How was it possible? Could one of them be his? He squeezed his daughter with love and stared in disbelief as Kari screamed and the doctor caught another baby as it slipped from her womb.

"Wha...what is't..." Kari gasped as she tried to regain her breath. Her face was flushed and beaded with sweat; her chest heaved up and down and her gasps were heavy and sonorous. The doctor carried their second baby around the corner, and Kari and

John saw that it was wrapped up in a blanket of blue wool.

"And it's a boy," the doctor said, handing the baby to Kari and plucking the gloves from his hands. Kari looked into the boy's eyes and it promptly began to bawl.

"Oh, dear dear..." she said, patting its head. It stopped crying and stared up at John, its little eyes unblinking.

"It has your eyes," the doctor commented. John looked from the baby to the doctor, then back again. It was true- the little human seemed to, in fact, look like a miniature of John. But it couldn't be. That wasn't possible.

"It's... it can't have my eyes," John said, handing the baby girl to Kari so that she could hold both her children at once. Kari smiled and her eyes closed.

"I love you, John," she said tiredly.

"I love you too, Kari," he said. He stared at the beautiful picture before him- his wife, holding their two children to her breasts, three lovely humans that were now a part of his life, forever. He felt tears well up in his eyes and he grinned as his wife and his two newborn children drifted off to sleep.

The doctor ushered him out of the room to go over some paperwork. As they neared the end of the paperwork, John stopped.

"Could we... um," he didn't exactly know how to phrase what he wanted to say; he wasn't even quite sure if he should ask it. "I know it is a stupid question," he began, "but can we possibly do a paternity test for the two children?"

The doctor eyed John, then nodded.

"Of course. Do you have doubts about the father?" he asked, his voice laced with guilt.

John shook his head, blushing.

"No," he said, "no. It's just- my wife was married before, and inseminated with her husband's frozen sperm before we met. But it was one baby, before we met. And I'm just wondering..." his voice trailed off as he realized how crazy the story sounded.

The doctor smiled stiffly and nodded his head.

"Alright. Sounds like a plan," he said. He shuffled some papers and slid a pen John's way. "Now if you'll just sign here..."

Chapter Seven

John spent every day with Kari and the children, as much as he could. He would teach his classes and then rush to the hospital, his heart light and full. As he went about his everyday life, he couldn't help but keep a smile from taking over his face. He was so, so in love with his two little children and his beautiful family. He wanted to hold them next to him forever and always; he wished he could take his two babies and his stunning wife to each and every lesson he had to teach! He couldn't wait for the day that they were allowed to leave the hospitals and take the babies home.

John rushed into the hospital clutching a bouquet to his chest. Just as he was about to press the button on the elevator to take him to the third floor, a nurse laid her hand gently upon his shoulder.

"John?" she asked. He turned to greet the nurse with whom he'd spoken quite a bit since Kari had given birth. He smiled, and she returned his expression. "They've completed the paternity test," she said. His eyes widened and he nodded, encouraging her to continue. "It's very interesting," she began, her brow creasing. "I think you'll be interested to take a look."

"Absolutely," John agreed. The nurse slid a paper from her pocket and handed it to him.

"As you can see, the girl's paternity seems to lie with your wife's late husband, Mark," she said, pointing a manicured fingernail to a string of digits along the top of the page. John squinted, then nodded.

"Yes," he said, "of course that makes sense. That's honestly what we expected." He began to return the paper to the nurse, blushing ever so slightly. It had been silly and wishful of him to think that he had played any part in creating the children.

But the nurse reached out a hand and stopped John before he could return the paper.

"But the son," she said, running her finger along a different line of digits inked along the bottom of the page, "seems to have a different father."

John's heart began to leap in his chest and he peered down at the results. His eyes widened and he felt his hands begin to shake as he read the words on the paper.

"You mean..." he said. He shook his head and stuttered. "Do you mean that means that..."

The nurse smiled up at him and shook his hand.

"Congratulations, John," she said. "You're a father."

Chapter Eight

"You were always the father," Kari said, her face full of light. Her cheeks were pink and her eyes were bright, and she looked calm, beautiful, and happy. Her two babies were nestled up against her chin as she breast fed them, and she grinned at John.

"I know," John said, pinching at his son's cheek. "I know. But still."

Kari blew a kiss at her husband.

"It's perfect," she said. She looked down at her two children and her eyes filled with tears. "Oh, John, it's all so perfect."

John pressed his lips against her forehead and lightly patted his two children. His daughter, and his son.

"It is perfect," he said. "But what do we call them?"

Kari pulled the babies from her breasts. She handed their son to John, and cradled their daughter in her arms.

"We can still call him Markus," John said, staring down into the baby's bright blue eyes. At the sound of the name, the little boy grinned and began to laugh. John chuckled back, and Kari giggled in amazement.

"Well that name seems to suit him well," John commented, rocking Markus back and forth.

Kari shook her head in disbelief and stared down at their little girl. Suddenly her face lit up and she grinned giddily up at her husband.

"I know what we should call her!" she cried.

John laughed at his wife's sheer, childlike excitement.

"Oh yea?" he teased. "What?"

Kari bit her lip and grinned, her face as beautiful as ever.

"We'll call her Evangeline," she said, "after your mother."

John felt love well up in his heart at the sound of his mother's name. It was perfect. And of course Kari had thought of it. She was the most beautiful, lovely human, inside and out. She had so much kindness in her heart, and was the most caring woman he had ever encountered. She would make the best mother for his children, and he knew his own mother would have been honored to know they were using her name.

"It's perfect," John said, smiling at his wife and daughter. He walked across the room to sit on the foot of the bed, rocking his son in his arms. He stared at the life that he had created in amazement. This little boy had been made purely out of the love he and Kari shared. These two tiny humans that were now so much a part of everything existed here today because two people had loved each other explosively.

Kari watched her husband hold their son, and her heart skipped and jumped in joy. She looked down at their daughter, and thought fondly of Mark. She knew he was looking down on them now, sending love and support and congratulations their way. She wished that John could have met Mark. They would have liked each other. They were very different people, but at the cores, they were alike- they were both loving, giving men that wanted nothing more than to brighten the lives of the people they cared for.

The doctor came in and wrote up the birth certificates, and Kari signed with a smile glued upon her face. John could not stop playing with his babies. He rocked them back and forth, sang to them in his off key, warbling bass voice, giggled as they grabbed at his fingers and spit up their milk. He kissed them on their little bellies; he pulled off their socks and laughed at their tiny toes; he laid them down to sleep and rubbed their backs. The whole time he held in his eyes the greatest look of love and gratitude. Kari watched him do all this and felt she might explode with thanks and love.

Finally, the babies settled down to sleep, and their slumbers lasted for more than an hour. John ran a hand over his face and helped Kari to move from the bed to the small table in the corner of the hospital room. John went to the cafeteria and bought them tuna sandwiches and orange juices, and they ate in the hospital room in silence, holding hands, as their babies slept on.

Kari finished her orange juice and looked across the table at her husband. His face was calm, content, and peaceful. John turned and caught Kari looking at him and grinned. Her face was pale and pink at the cheeks, and her lips were bright and full. He thought that he loved her very, very much, and was so grateful that he had thrown a fit about the cupcakes, so many months ago.

Kari wouldn't stop looking at him. She suddenly burst into laughter, and John started laughing too, caught off guard.

"What is it?" he asked, his mouth curved into a smile. "What?"

Kari shook her head. Then she stood up, and pulled a small white box from beneath the bed.

John arched an eyebrow as Kari handed him the box. She grinned guiltily and admitted, "I got Mary to bring it while you were teaching lessons today."

John placed the box on his lap and slowly opened it. There, inside, was a perfect cupcake, iced with purple frosting, topped with an intricate design of sparkles and pearls. It was the exact identical to the cupcake he'd thrown a fit about on the first day he and Kari had met.

He looked up at her and burst out laughing. She began to laugh too, and threw her arms around his shoulders. He picked up the cupcake and took a bite. It was sweet, but not too sweet, beautiful, but not tacky. It was everything Kari was, and everything John wanted his life to be.

He caught his wife still staring at him as he polished off the cupcake. He licked his fingers and offered her the last few bites. She popped the sweet, purply cake into her mouth and grinned.

"What?" he asked. "What are you thinking of, staring at me like that?"

She bit her laugh and smiled.

"Oh, nothing," she said. "Just that I love you so much."

John smiled back.

"And I, you."

Kari giggled, and kept chewing. But John could see there was something more on her mind.

"And..." he prompted.

Kari shifted her weight and swallowed.

"Well," she began. "After I lost Mark, I remember thinking it was going to be so hard. To find love, to have a child, to... well, to live." She grabbed his hand. "But then I met you. And you know what?"
"What?" John asked.

"Well, quite simply," Kari continued, "I learned the truth. Life is hard. It is. But do you know what happens if you find the right person?"

John looked at her, his eyes of love. To their left, their babies yawned and burped. Everything was perfect.

"What happens," he asked, "if you find the right person?"

Kari grinned.

"If you find the right person, John," she said, "then everything becomes just how we met: like a piece of cake."

END

www.ingramcontent.com/pod-product-compliance
Lightning Source LLC
LaVergne TN
LVHW041637070526
838199LV00052B/3423